The Melting Pot

An Adventure in New York

The Do-It-Yourself
Jewish Adventure series

THE CARDINAL'S SNUFFBOX
by Kenneth Roseman

THE MELTING POT:
An Adventure in New York
by Kenneth Roseman

The Melting Pot

An Adventure in New York

Kenneth Roseman

• • •

Union of American Hebrew Congregations
New York

Photographs, courtesy the American Jewish Archives,
Hebrew Union College-Jewish Institute of Religion
(cover, pp. 8, 12, 16, 23, 44); University of Minnesota Social Welfare History Archive (p. 64); Israel Government
Tourist Office (p. 79); Jewish National Fund (p. 97); Museum of the City of New York (pp. 104, 110).

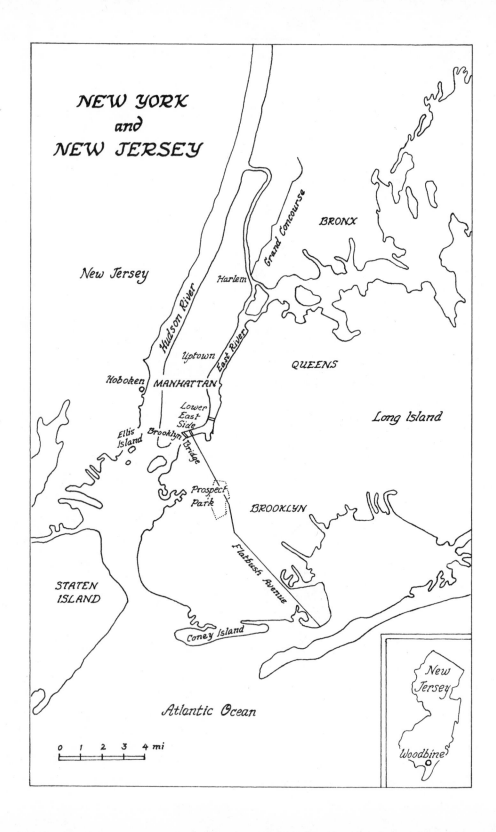

NEW YORK
and
NEW JERSEY

New Jersey

BRONX

Grand Concourse

Hudson River

Harlem

East River

Uptown

QUEENS

Hoboken MANHATTAN

Lower
East
Side

Long Island

Ellis
Island

Brooklyn Bridge

Prospect
Park

BROOKLYN

STATEN
ISLAND

Flatbush Avenue

Coney Island

Atlantic Ocean

0 1 2 3 4 mi

New
Jersey

Woodbine

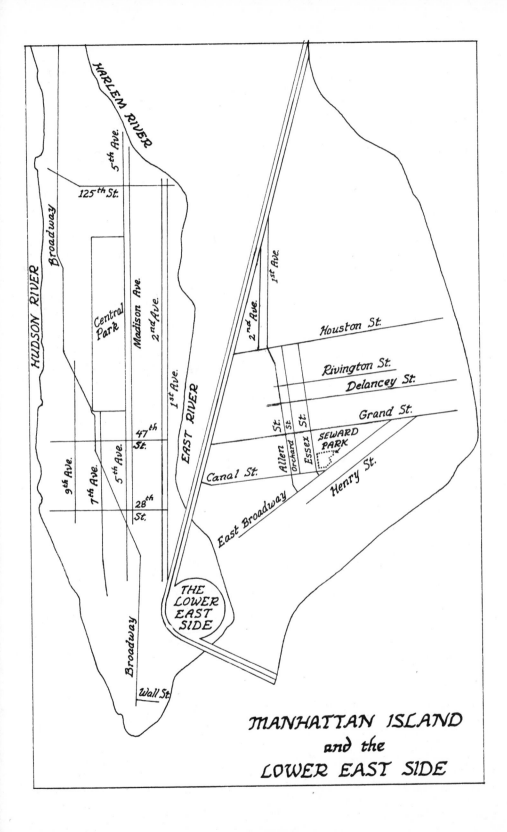

MANHATTAN ISLAND
and the
LOWER EAST SIDE

The Melting Pot

An Adventure in New York

1

You are about to read a very different kind of book. With most books, you start on page 1 and then turn to page 2, page 3, and so on, in sequence.

As you read this book, you'll proceed differently. Read the first seven pages. At the bottom of page 7, you will be asked to make a choice. If you decide one way, the instructions tell you to turn to page 8; if you elect the other option, you will go to page 9. Almost every page thereafter asks you to make a choice.

After you have read to the end of one series of choices, you can go back to an earlier part of the book and find out what would have happened if you had chosen differently.

There are many different stories in this book.

2

This book is historical fiction. The events you will read about are based on facts; the characters you will meet are real; the problems and the choices you will face were once faced by those real people. You may want to look in an atlas or refer to the maps included in this book as you read. That way, you can follow your journey as you make your choices.

The careful reader will notice that some of the events in this book occurred farther apart or closer together in history than here. Of course, what you will read about could not have happened to just one person. These events have been condensed into one person's life so that you could have more choices and more fun as you create your own adventures.

As you come across words in italics, look them up in the glossary at the back of the book. Please note that we have used the Sephardic pronunciation of Hebrew words throughout the book, even though the Ashkenazic pronunciation was characteristic of Eastern European Jews.

Now, turn to page 3.

3

Early one evening, you and your mother and father, your three sisters and four brothers are sitting in the one small room of your home. Though Papa and Mama work very hard, there is barely enough money for food, clothing, and a little *tsedakah* for those even poorer than you. You live in the *shtetl* of *Kapulia,* located near the Russian city of Minsk. It is cold this March day, but the lane outside has already thawed enough to become a pool of mud.

You are reading the *haftarah* that will be chanted by the *Bar Mitzvah* next *Shabbat* and from time to time you help your younger brother with his *cheder* lessons. Your mother is teaching two of your sisters to sew.

You remember clearly, as though it was yesterday, a knock at the door that changed your life.

4

It was Yankel, the postman. Your family had not received any mail since last *Sukot,* so everyone excitedly gathered around to hear Papa read the unexpected letter. Mama looked up from her glass of tea, sugar cube clenched between her teeth.

"Sha! Still!" Papa ordered, getting you to quiet down. Then, he began to read.

Tayerhar Mishpocheh,
I have lived in this golden land for three years now. Of course, I miss all of you very much, but America is special. Everyday, I work at a sewing machine, making shirts, earning six dollars a week. Can you believe it? Six whole dollars! There is a large *shul* which I attend on *Shabbat.*

Your oldest child is now thirteen, old enough to join me here. There is much work available and a far better life. The future for Jews in America is very good. Please consider this carefully. I shall care for your child as for my own. Enclosed is enough money to pay for the ticket.
Love,
Cousin Hyman

5

The decision is a difficult one. Your parents argue about it for days. Finally, on the following Sabbath eve, after the candles have been lit, the *Shabbat Kiddush* chanted, and the *chalah* cut, Papa makes the announcement.

"Cousin Hyman is right. The future for us under the *tsar* is black. From day to day, we live in fear of a *pogrom*. Who knows whether we shall live or die? My child," he says to you, "you will go to America. We do not know whether we shall see you again, but we have no choice. We must think of your future. As your brothers and sisters grow older, they will join you."

The next morning, during *Shabbat* services, the rabbi makes a *Mi Sheberach,* asking God's protection for you. When the holy day has ended, you and Papa take the money Cousin Hyman has sent and buy your passage—first by cart with a farmer from *Kapulia* to Warsaw, then by train to Berlin and the port city of Hamburg, and finally by steamship with hundreds of others to New York.

6

The morning of your departure, you cry and you are afraid. After all, you have never been more than one hour's walk from home. Everyone kisses and hugs you, then kisses you again, and finally gives you one last kiss and goodbye. The cart driver calls to you, and you climb aboard. Three other young people from your *shtetl* are traveling with you.

The ride is long and tiring. Twice, you push the cart out of deep mud. The train is not much better—hot and crowded, filled with other young Jews from the *Pale of Settlement,* all fleeing to the land of hope and promise. At Hamburg, you board the ship and are directed to a crowded steerage hold. There, in a dark and smelly corner, you set your belongings down. Your suitcase will be your pillow and the floor your mattress for the next twelve days.

Food and sanitation on the boat are terrible, but the days pass, and soon you land at *Ellis Island.* Immigration officials examine you for disease and question you in a language you do not understand to make sure that you have enough money on which to live. Fortunately, a representative from the *Hebrew Immigrant Aid Society* helps you answer the questions. He even knows Cousin Hyman! Finally, you are permitted to take the ferry across the harbor to New York City. You have arrived in America!

Cousin Hyman meets you with a hearty *"Shalom."* You go with him to the Lower East Side of the city where hundreds of thousands of immigrant Jews like yourself live. The streets are filled with peddlers and pushcarts selling everything from clothing to food, buttons to furniture, shoes to wigs. It is so crowded you can hardly push your way through.

At the corner of Rivington and Essex streets, Cousin Hyman leads you into a *tenement* building and up four flights of stairs. Inside the apartment, two men are sleeping on the floor. Cousin Hyman makes you a good meal, and then on a narrow cot you sleep soundly for the first time since you left Russia.

With the sunrise, you dress and decide to explore the neighborhood. You quickly realize this is an exciting place with much to see and do. You are sure that your trip to New York City was *bashert,* that God had intended you to come and that it is here you must stay.

At dinner, you tell Cousin Hyman, and he agrees. "But," he says, "we've got to find you some way to make a living. You saw the carts yesterday; perhaps my friend, Amiel, could help you get started as a street-corner vendor. On the other hand, you could come with me to the sweatshop and learn to sew clothing."

If you decide to become a pushcart vendor, turn to page 8.

If you decide to work at the sweatshop, turn to page 9.

8

The busiest street in the neighborhood is Orchard Street. The pushcart Amiel helps you rent sells meat. All day long, you stand on the corner and yell: *"Fleish! Frishe fleish! Glat kosher fleish!"* It's hard work, getting up at five in the morning to get the meat from the slaughterhouse and staying out until dark, but it pays off. Slowly, week by week, month by month, you save your earnings, until you have more money than you ever dreamed of.

One evening, you take Cousin Hyman aside. "I've saved my money, just like you told me to do. Now, I have $50. There is a butcher on Grand Street who wants a partner. Maybe I should continue in the meat business. On the other hand, you know clothing. If I bought a sewing machine, we could make women's corsets together."

*If you decide to become a butcher,
turn to page 11.*

*If you buy a sewing machine,
turn to page 12.*

9

You climb seven flights of stairs to the loft of a large building. In an immense room, hundreds of women are working at sewing machines. Young men move about the room, making sure each seamstress has the proper materials, collecting the pieces she has finished. Supervisors count each woman's production to determine her pay.

You are assigned to a section where the sleeves of shirtwaist dresses are sewed. You arrive at work at seven in the morning and, with the exception of a half-hour for lunch, you continue until six in the evening. During the winter, the loft is bitterly cold; in the summer, the heat is unbearable, and people faint. Those that do get paid less for producing less.

You realize that the only people who make money are the contractors who hire the other workers. One of your co-workers tells you the sewing machine operators will always be poor unless the labor union does something about it.

If you decide to become a contractor,
turn to page 13.

If you are upset about the slave-like conditions
and want to join a labor union,
turn to page 14.

10

You become quickly convinced that *socialism* will never work. People in America just don't seem interested in making society more just. All they want is more money and power for themselves. You wonder whether you can continue to live in such a selfish society.

Maybe it was a mistake to come here, especially when the working class in Russia has just overthrown the *tsar*. In Russia, you would have a better chance to improve life, and you could see your parents again.

On the other hand, perhaps you should stay in America. You take a long walk to clear your head.

If you walk on Second Avenue,
turn to page 16.

If you walk along Broadway,
turn to page 17.

If you decide to go back to Europe
and join the Communist Revolution,
turn to page 15.

11

The meat you and your partner peddle together is, of course, *kosher*. Most Jews on the Lower East Side are very poor. They often must work on *Shabbat* simply to survive. But many of them still try to maintain the Jewish religious laws and traditions, and keeping *kosher* is one of the most important to them.

One day, the *Yiddish* newspapers in the neighborhood carry a headline: "*Treif* meat sold as *kosher*." You had heard rumors that some dishonest butchers had bought cheaper, non-*kosher* meat and were selling it as *kosher*. But you had told your partner, "That would be like cheating God!"

Now, angry customers demand that every butcher, even the honest ones, submit to a new system of inspection. They want an independent authority to guarantee that meat sold as *kosher* really is. Some people propose that New York's chief rabbi, *Jacob Joseph,* be put in charge. Others think that *Tammany Hall,* the local political organization, can solve the problem. It's one or the other. Your customers insist on satisfaction.

If you go with them to the chief rabbi,
turn to page 19.

If all of you agree on Tammany Hall,
turn to page 20.

12

Y ou place your new sewing machine in the front room of Cousin Hyman's apartment. For twelve to fourteen hours each day you make corsets, sewing together fabric you get from the contractor down the street. After dark, you carry the finished products to the contractor and pick up new materials for the next day.

Through hard work, you are able to buy more machines, and before very long you have your own small factory. At first, everything goes well, and you make a profit. But then the cost of the fabric goes up, and you can hardly make enough money to pay your workers.

Perhaps you should sell the machines. You've always wanted to be a farmer, and recently you learned of a Jewish farming settlement in Woodbine, N.J.

If you decide to try farming,
turn to page 21.

If you continue with your corset factory,
turn to page 22.

13

Saving your money, you purchase a few sewing machines. At first, you work in Cousin Hyman's apartment. But eventually you need to expand. You must open your own garment factory. Growing larger means finding a new location for your workshop and possibly being forced to work on *Shabbat*—something you were always taught Jews did not do.

If you choose to ignore observing Shabbat, turn to page 23.

If you prefer to keep your traditional religious observance, turn to page 24.

14

Jewish workers in the clothing industry have founded two unions: the *International Ladies Garment Workers' Union* (ILGWU) for women's clothing and the *Amalgamated Clothing Workers of America* for men's. As you are choosing which group to work for, you hear reports of a terrible fire at the *Triangle Shirtwaist Company.* Over a hundred people have died, mostly because the building in which they worked was overcrowded and had inadequate fire escapes.

You meet with *Morris Hillquit,* the representative of the ILGWU, and offer your help in working to improve conditions. *Mr. Hillquit* gratefully accepts your assistance. "Things have got to change," he says. "The sweatshop bosses can no longer treat workers like trash!"

Most of the union leadership wants to call a strike to force employers to improve working conditions and wages. Everyone understands that a strike would be very hard on the workers, but it might help in the long run.

If you agree to join the strike,
turn to page 25.

If you believe there is an easier way
to secure better working conditions,
turn to page 26.

15

The news from Russia excites you. "The *Messiah* must be right around the corner," you tell your friends. "I've got to get back to the Old Country and take part in the liberation of my people."

You board a ship and, a few weeks later, step onto the dock at Leningrad. A group of soldiers wearing red *Communist* armbands greets you. "I'm here to help the revolution," you explain. "No, you aren't," they respond. "You are a spy from our enemies." They stand you up against a building, blindfold you, and a firing squad executes you.

E N D

16

As you walk on Second Avenue, you see a row of theaters. Posters in front of them advertize familiar names: *Boris Thomashefsky, Abraham Goldfaden, Jacob Gordin, Muni Weisenfreund, Molly Picon, Jacob Adler,* and dozens of other Jewish actors and actresses. The plays are all in *Yiddish.* Thousands of Lower East Side residents come to see the performances every day—except *Shabbat.*

"This is the place for me," you shout out loud. You enter the *Grand Theatre* and secure a job as a stagehand. You put politics behind you and settle for a career in the creative and artistic world of dramatic arts.

END

17

Your path leads you up Broadway and across 28th Street to the area in Manhattan known as *Tin Pan Alley*. From every side, you hear the sounds of music. *Alma Gluck, Rosa Ponselle, Sophie Braslau,* and *Leonard Warren* are practicing operatic arias. *Gus Kahn, Ira* and *George Gershwin, Richard Rodgers,* and *Oscar Hammerstein II* are working on new compositions, while violinists, pianists, and other musicians add their own notes to the symphony.

The lovely music makes you stop and think. A country in which Jews can be such leaders in the cultural world cannot be so bad after all. You retrace your steps and return to the Lower East Side. In this land, you will make your future. For better or for worse, you are now an American.

END

18

You buy an apartment building and move in as manager. Because you remember how difficult it was to be a stranger, moving to a new place, you treat your tenants well. They appreciate your kindness, pay their rents on time, and help keep your building clean.

With the additional money you earn from this building, you purchase others until you own four fine apartment houses. You are known as a fair and honest owner, and people respect you.

One day, two groups come to you with business propositions. One delegation represents the *International Ladies Garment Workers' Union* (ILGWU). The other group comes from a landlords' association on the Lower East Side.

If you meet with the ILGWU,
turn to page 27.

If you prefer to meet with the landlords,
turn to page 28.

19

The office of the chief rabbi is crowded and hot. People are yelling accusations back and forth. Everyone has something to say.

Finally, *Rabbi Jacob Joseph* gives his decision. "I believe that you are an honest butcher. But public confidence must be restored. People must be able to trust that the word *'kosher'* means exactly that. Therefore, you will pay a tax of two cents per pound of meat and one cent per pound of chicken. The money will be used to pay for the inspector I shall send to your shop."

You and your partner have no choice but to agree. But paying this tax means your products will cost more than those of other butchers. You ask your customers to be loyal to you, but poor people usually shop where the price is less. Soon, the income from your shop declines, and you are faced with deciding whether to continue in business or to close your doors.

If you continue,
turn to page 35.

If you close the store,
turn to page 36.

20

At *Tammany Hall,* you and your customers meet with several politicians. Many are Irish and smoke large cigars. They seem to know how to solve every situation. After a long conference, they tell you what will happen. "Your customers really do trust you, and, more than that, they trust us to keep you honest. As long as you sell truly *kosher* meat, there will be no problem. If you try to cheat, the police will close you down—permanently!"

To insure the friendship of the political bosses, you promise to make a monthly contribution to the *Democratic party.* That payment helps protect your store and allows you to stay in business. In fact, when your new relationship with *Tammany Hall* becomes known, more people buy your meats, and you prosper.

You begin to think. If *Tammany Hall* is so powerful, maybe you should work for them. They did offer you a good position! But your butcher shop is thriving.

If you go to work for the political organization, turn to page 37.

If you keep your own business and expand it, turn to page 38.

21

The small town of Woodbine is located about 140 miles south of New York City. You arrive by train and take a horse-drawn wagon to the Jewish farm. Most of the people are like you, recent immigrants who want to get away from the big city and shopkeeping.

You are assigned to plant vegetables and hoe the crops as they grow and ripen. Working the soil of the fields with your hands feels good, and you sweat; but fatigue is an honest, healthy feeling. Yet, despite your new sense of accomplishment, you aren't fully satisfied. Something is missing.

"It's simply a matter of time," you tell yourself. "Another few months, and I'll feel at home here." But the nagging feeling lingers. One day, you hear that the best Jewish farmers live on *kibbutzim* in Palestine. Perhaps that is where you belong and you should make *aliyah* to Palestine.

If you decide to stay in Woodbine,
turn to page 39.

If you decide to make aliyah to Palestine,
turn to page 40.

22

Your decision to continue in the corset business carries a good deal of risk. You have stretched your assets to the limit; one more piece of bad news and you may lose everything.

Then, the fashion designers on Seventh Avenue in Manhattan create a new image for women's clothing. The "healthy," robust look is out; women are now supposed to look as slender as possible. Overnight, your corset business expands as women seek ways to make their waistlines look smaller. The more corsets are sold, the more your bank account increases.

The demand for corsets is so heavy that you consider expanding the business. You'll have to borrow money and accept some additional risks, but it looks quite encouraging to do so.

But, at dinner, Cousin Hyman suggests selling the corset factory at a profit and urges you to go into the real estate business, owning and managing large buildings. He also reminds you that you always wanted to go to college.

If you decide to expand your business,
turn to page 41.

If you decide to go to college,
turn to page 42.

If you decide to enter the real estate business,
turn to page 18.

23

After several years of struggle, you are now the head of a large clothing factory. You look out over the workroom and smile with satisfaction.

Your workers, however, are not so happy. Their working conditions are terrible, and they are distressed about being required to work on *Shabbat.* At first, they air their dissatisfaction among themselves. Then, they send a delegation to present their complaints directly to you. You explain to them that you cannot run your business based on what the employees want. If they want better conditions, they are free to find new jobs.

The delegation storms out of your office, informs the other workers of your attitude, and decides to call a strike. Everyone walks off the job. It could cost you your entire business if it continues for a long time.

If you decide to settle the strike,
turn to page 43.

If you refuse to give in to the workers,
turn to page 44.

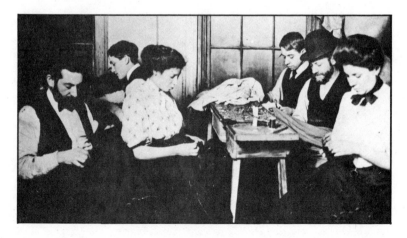

24

Being your own boss, no one can force you to give up your religious way of life. During the few recesses you take from running your shop, you read a *Yiddish* newspaper, the *Forvarts*. Its editor, *Abraham Cahan,* describes the ways in which the capitalist bosses of industry and finance take advantage of their workers. The paper also tells of their Fifth Avenue mansions in the loveliest part of Manhattan, their luxurious parties, and their fancy vacations.

Even though you own your business, you do not fit into that category. You know you should resent these capitalists but, instead, you envy them. This is the way you would like to live. And why not? You are as smart as they are! You've already got a good start; you've got your own business; but it is only a small step toward becoming the capitalist you want to be.

If you decide to become such a capitalist,
turn to page 45.

If the risk of running a big business frightens you,
turn to page 46.

25

The strike lasts for months. Pickets block the entrance of each factory with signs, while the owners hire *scab* workers to cross the picket lines and keep the factories running. Each side tries to make life as difficult as possible for the other side, in the hope that someone will finally give in.

The suffering on both sides is great. The owners discover that few people will defy the union. Factories go out of business permanently because the owners can no longer pay their bills. At the same time, the striking workers have little or no money to buy food, fuel, clothing, and other necessities for their families.

As you witness the misery caused by the strike, you think: "Perhaps it's not worth it. Maybe we should settle the dispute and put the workers back on the job." On the other hand, success requires sacrifice. This would mean that you will hold out.

If you decide to settle,
turn to page 47.

If you decide to continue the strike,
turn to page 48.

26

Among the working people in New York, there are many different ideas about how to improve conditions. Everywhere you go, groups of people are arguing about the right path to follow.

The *Socialist party,* working peacefully within the political system, wants to take the factories away from the capitalists and give them to the workers. "Why should one person make profits from our work," they argue. "Let the workers own the means of production and share the profits equally!"

A much smaller, radical group disagrees. "The owners will never give in," they exclaim. "The only way for us to gain control is by violent revolution. Throw out the capitalists! *Workers of the world, unite!"*

If you decide to join the Socialists,
turn to page 49.

If you agree with the radicals,
turn to page 50.

27

The union representatives tell you a sad story. Most of the ILGWU members are Jewish and live on the Lower East Side. Because they are poor, these workers cannot afford good health care. They become ill with tuberculosis and other diseases; many children die at birth or in infancy. No one ever sees a dentist.

They propose to you that the ground floor of one of your buildings be converted into a neighborhood health center. The ILGWU and you will share the cost of paying a doctor, a nurse, and a dentist who will treat poor people for free or for whatever they can afford.

It's a *mitzvah* that you cannot refuse. These are your people; they need your help. The papers are signed, and the project is undertaken. On opening day, a surprise awaits you. A plaque is unveiled naming the health center in your honor. As poor people flood into the clinic, you feel gratified and smile with satisfaction.

E N D

28

The landlords offer you a package of twelve *tenement* apartment buildings. Their price is so low and the opportunity for large profits so great that you cannot resist. Putting up your other buildings as security, you borrow the necessary funds and buy these *tenements*.

Several months later, you wish you had been more careful. The conditions in the buildings are terrible. No one lives there willingly, and those who do rarely can afford to pay their rent. The building inspector threatens to close up the buildings unless you make major repairs. Your good reputation has been destroyed. You are now known as a "slumlord." You are trapped in a dilemma with no hope of escape. Because of your bad judgment, you eventually lose everything.

END

29

You decide to open a jewelry store on 47th Street in Manhattan's diamond center. There are many rich people living nearby who purchase fine gems. Upstairs from the store, you employ *Orthodox Jews* who cut the gem stones and mount them in rings, bracelets, and necklaces.

Your reputation as an honest and fair dealer spreads, and customers flock to your store. You are convinced that your remaining closed on *Shabbat* has something to do with your success, so you make an extra donation to the *shul* to show your appreciation.

Three other small diamond merchants on your street approach you one day and suggest a partnership. "This street," they believe, "could be the diamond capital of the Americas."

If you are content with your own good business, turn to page 31.

If you decide to enter into a partnership with them, turn to page 32.

30

One doesn't become a stockbroker overnight. Your first step is to take night-school courses in business and finance while you keep your small business and run your workshop during the day. Eventually, you are able to get a job as a stockbroker in the firm of *Kuhn, Loeb and Company* and you sell your workshop and your sewing machines.

Working in the stock market, you consult with people who are trying to raise money for their businesses. They use the capital they receive from selling stock to improve their products and expand their market. You also invest your own money wisely and gradually accumulate a modest fortune. You raise a family and send your children to good schools.

One of the companies you work with is exploring for oil. The prospects look good, and you think you might invest in the venture yourself. You have never done something like this; it's very risky, but the chance to make a great deal of money is hard to ignore.

If you stick to your established, "safe" style, turn to page 33.

If you invest in the oil stock, turn to page 34.

31

What the other three businessmen didn't tell you was that they were in serious financial trouble. When they go bankrupt, you realize how fortunate you were in not being greedy.

You arrange a meeting with them and offer to buy what is left of their merchandise. "Ten cents on the dollar," you offer, "and I'm being generous at that, after what you tried to do to me!"

They accept, and now you control a large part of New York's diamond center. Nothing can stop your success now. All at once, you are a millionaire, and your dream of becoming a Fifth Avenue capitalist has come true.

END

32

The expansion sours, right from the start. You've undertaken too much; there are not enough customers to pay the bills. Even your relatives, who gladly loaned you money when your future looked bright, now want to be repaid—but you haven't got any money. Your new partners aren't any help; in fact, they brought their own problems into the business and made matters worse.

You declare bankruptcy and cannot even start another business because your credit is bad and you have lost your good reputation. You spend the rest of your life working for other people.

END

33

Your reputation as a cautious and conservative investment advisor serves you well. You are promoted from stockbroker to junior partner and eventually to senior partner— quite an achievement for a poor immigrant.

You hear of the prestigious *Harmonie Club* and apply for membership, but the Jewish club rejects you. You believe that being an *Eastern European Jew* had to do with the rejection. The pain you suffer is similar to the pain you feel when non-Jewish clients ask to deal with someone "who is more like we are." Even though you've come a long way, you still haven't completely gained social acceptance.

But you also feel certain that you've paved the way for your children who will be able to gain that complete acceptance in society, and you feel good about even this partial achievement.

E N D

34

A messenger comes into your office with a telegram. Your fingers tremble as you open it. You read with anxiety: "After finding oil storm blows rig over. Fire destroys everything."

You are ruined. All your money has been pledged for the stock, and, now, the stock is worthless. The blow is too much for you, and you have a heart attack. For a month, you fight for your life. When you recover, the doctor strongly urges you to accept early retirement. "After all," you're told, "what's a few more years of work compared to living long enough to see your grandchildren grow up?"

The doctor has a point and you can't argue. To recuperate and to step completely away from working, you rent an apartment in Florida for January and February.

Turn to page 51.

35

Staying in business is not easy; it's rather a struggle. You are as poor as most of your customers. As time passes, you marry someone from a town near yours in the Old Country, and you have a family, two sons and a daughter. Even though you and your spouse work, it hardly seems enough to cover all your expenses.

When you look around at your friends, you notice that they are not as poor as you are. In fact, one after another, they are leaving the Lower East Side and moving *uptown* to a new Jewish neighborhood called *Harlem*. Many Jews, of course, remain on the Lower East Side; but you and your family miss your friends and would like a better life like theirs. It would be difficult and risky to try to start your butcher shop elsewhere; you might lose even the little you have. It certainly would be safer to stay where you are, but you aren't doing well at all.

You and your spouse spend long hours debating the choice. Finally, you both reach a conclusion.

If you decide to remain on the Lower East Side, turn to page 68.

If you conclude that you must move to Harlem, turn to page 69.

36

You spend several long evenings trying to figure out a way to avoid closing the shop. You add long columns of numbers, showing prices, pounds of meat, tax due, and other expenses and finally conclude: there is no way that the butcher shop will survive with the new tax. Equally true, there is no way you will sell meat unless it is *kosher.* Your partner shares your feelings and accepts your decision.

You close down the business. You will surely miss talking with your customers, and the poor Jewish widows and children will miss getting the trimmings from the meat that you gave them anonymously. You must now find something new to do.

Secretly, you've always wanted to continue your education. After all, what higher goal can a person have than to become a scholar! Two avenues are open to you. You could either enroll in the preparatory program of the *Jewish Theological Seminary of America* (JTS) and study to become a *Conservative* rabbi, or you could attend night school at the *City College of New York* (CCNY). If you go to CCNY, you will have to work all day, but you could study any subject you wanted to.

If you enroll at JTS,
turn to page 70.

If you select CCNY,
turn to page 42.

37

Working for *Tammany Hall* gives you great satisfaction. You find many ways to use the organization's power to help people secure jobs, housing, coal, food, and other necessities. When something bad happens to a person in your ward, you can often ease the difficulties. Sometimes, you think you are able to do more than the government to assist new immigrants, and you feel especially good about helping other immigrant Jews.

Your effective work gains you the recognition of the *Tammany Hall* leadership, who promote you to head the "Commercial Division" and grant you a huge raise in pay. But something about the way they talk worries you. They are very secretive, as if trying to cover up a crime. If *Tammany Hall* is involved in criminal activities, you might be implicated. Maybe you should resign and go to work for the political party trying to defeat the *Tammany Hall* bosses.

If you accept the "Commercial Division" position, turn to page 90.

If you decide to run on the reform ticket, turn to page 73.

38

The bosses at *Tammany Hall* understand your decision. "After all," they tell you, "everyone's got to eat. Besides, you've been our friend and have been giving a contribution to our treasury every week or so."

With the encouragement of the political organization and your own synagogue and community contacts, your butcher shop continues to prosper. As profits increase, your bank account grows. You wonder how you should invest the money. One possibility would be to start another business. On the other hand, you could expand your butcher shop, adding new types of products.

If you choose to diversify, turn to page 59.

If you prefer to expand, turn to page 60.

39

On *Shabbat* afternoon, all the farmers are summoned to an important meeting at the community center. *David Lubin* is to speak. "Who is this person?" you ask, as you walk toward the meeting.

"Why, he's just about the most important agricultural reformer and organizer in the world! *Victor Emanuel II,* king of Italy, favored his plan to establish the *International Institute of Agriculture* and made him head of it."

You are impressed. *Lubin* looks like any other middle-aged man, but he speaks forcefully. "You must plant new types of crops," he urges. "I suggest carrots and red cabbage. They will grow well here. If you truck them to New York and Philadelphia where people need them, you will make a good deal of money, and you'll be feeding lots of hungry folks."

"He's right," you think. "We've got to branch out and experiment." You volunteer to plant one of the new crops . . . but which one?

If you select carrots,
turn to page 76.

If you choose red cabbage,
turn to page 77.

40

Having decided to make *aliyah* and spend the rest of your life working on a *kibbutz,* you take a train back to New York. There, you discuss your plans with a group of *Zionists* who are also thinking about moving to Palestine. Excitement is everywhere. You are fulfilling a very old Jewish dream to return and rebuild the *Holy Land.*

Some people advise you to take a ship across the Atlantic Ocean to France and then go overland across Europe to Palestine. Others think you should buy passage on a ship that will take you as far as Italy and from there go on to the *Promised Land.*

If you take a ship bound for France,
turn to page 79.

If you buy a ticket for Italy,
turn to page 80.

41

You borrow money from the bank and move your factory to a larger building. One hundred people now work for you, sewing, packing, counting, shipping. . . . You spend long hours at the factory, watching every step, making sure there is no waste.

One day, one of your friends tells you there is a good buy on whalebone, flexible pieces of bone used to stiffen the sides of the corsets you make. Another corset maker was not as prudent in business as you and has gone broke. He will sell you his supply of whalebone for ten cents on the dollar. It's a good deal; you buy the entire stock.

If you put it away for some future use, hoping to make a "killing," a huge profit, turn to page 81.

If you use it immediately in your corsets, turn to page 82.

42

You do odd jobs during the day and enroll for night courses at *City College of New York.* You work very hard at your studies because it is a privilege to be able to go to college. In Russia, Jews were not allowed to enter the universities, and, even in America, only a very small percentage of the people continue past high school. You also remember what your father taught you: *"The study of wisdom is equal to all the rest of God's commandments."* Jews have always valued learning.

After two years, the dean sends for you and tells you: "Your academic record shows you have done very well, but now is the time to select a major subject to study. There are several areas of specialization that might be appropriate for you. You must make a selection in the next few days."

If you say you want to study philosophy,
turn to page 83.

If you decide on medical studies,
turn to page 84.

If law is your choice,
turn to page 85.

43

On *Yom Kippur,* as you sit in the synagogue, the words of the *Al Chet* prayer suddenly seem full of personal meaning —you realize that you have not been following the traditional teaching of Judaism. Perhaps you should settle the strike.

After *Neilah,* you approach the strike leaders. "Let's get together tomorrow," you say, "and see if we can work this out."

At your meeting the next day, the leaders present you with a list of terms they think will be acceptable. You ask for a day to think them over.

If you accept the terms,
turn to page 98.

If you reject them,
turn to page 99.

44

You tell the union committee that there will be no more talks while the strike continues. Even the famous labor negotiator, *Louis D. Brandeis,* cannot change your mind. No union is going to force you to give up what you worked so hard to achieve. You threaten to fire all striking workers. "There are many people just waiting to get good jobs like these," you tell them.

The pickets with their strike signs move from your business to your home. They stand outside, day and night, blocking your door, chanting slogans, making your life miserable. You and your family are virtually prisoners in your own home. You've got to do something.

If you sneak out in the middle of the night,
turn to page 100.

If you decide to call the police for help,
turn to page 101.

45

All you have is a few sewing machines in a comparatively small workshop—certainly not enough to start a big business and become the capitalist of Fifth Avenue. You need more money, more capital.

You buy a brand new suit at a store on Orchard Street and some accessories from the *Chasidim* on Allen Street. Now, you look like a real business executive. You arrange an appointment with the loan officer at a bank *uptown* and describe your plans. Everything seems to be alright until you mention how little money you have. "I'm sorry," is the answer, "but we cannot help you." Disappointed, you try the *Mutual Alliance Trust Company* in your neighborhood at Grand and Orchard streets. You hope you'll get more consideration from a bank directed by Jews. But the answer is still "No." Business is business among bankers, and no one will take a chance on you.

You won't take "No" for an answer, however. One way or another, you will be that big capitalist.

If you borrow from your friends and relatives, turn to page 29.

If you become a stockbroker and manage people's money, turn to page 30.

46

A neighbor of yours tried to become a businessman. He borrowed money and opened a clothing store. At first, you wished you had made the same choice. Later, when he lost all his money and had to accept charity to feed his family, you concluded that your decision was the correct one, after all. You decide to sell your few sewing machines and get out of the garment business altogether.

While you are thinking about your future, other people in your *tenement* tell you that Sam Levi, the delicatessen owner, has died. He was a good and gentle old man. You go to his funeral and, after the *shivah,* you visit Mrs. Levi. She no longer wants her husband's restaurant and proposes that you buy it.

Operating a deli, however, could have its problems. You remember your neighbor who risked all his money and went broke. Perhaps you should set a more modest goal and find a secure job with the City of New York.

If you decide to buy the deli,
turn to page 104.

If you apply for training in the police force,
turn to page 105.

47

You sit quietly in your synagogue on *Shabbat* morning. All around you, Jews are *davening*, but you are wrapped in thought. On the one hand, you are an officer of the ILGWU, and that means that you must fight for the rights of the workers, even if it causes hardship in their lives. But you are also a Jew. The *chazan* is reading from the *Torah*, and a phrase catches your attention—*Uvacharta ba-chayim*, "And you shall choose life."

You realize that, above all, life is precious and that you had made the right decision wanting to arrange a settlement. When *Shabbat* is over, you meet with the executive committee of the union. They agree to settle the strike. Later, they discuss future strategy for the labor union movement.

If you decide that labor unions won't work out,
turn to page 112.

If you decide the strike failed because of bad preparation,
and not because unions are wrong,
turn to page 102.

48

You counsel the workers to hold out. Just a few more days, you tell them, and the owners will surely surrender. The owners also understand that they cannot survive if the strike continues much longer. They hire thugs to beat you up, hoping to frighten the workers into ending the strike. Word comes to you, warning you that these toughs are headed your way.

If you run and hide,
turn to page 103.

If you stay and fight,
turn to page 88.

49

You join the *Socialist party* and keep working and organizing small groups to talk about the ideas of the party. You speak in public on many occasions. You believe that the rallies, speeches, and newspapers are effective. More people sign up to work for the cause.

With others, you debate the best way to push the *Socialist* cause. Some think that it should be done mainly through the Jewish community; others think that you should address the larger, general population. It's a difference of tactics: stay with a small, but committed group or expand the membership and risk attracting dead weight, people who won't do their share of the work.

If you decide to confine your message to the Jewish community,
turn to page 89.

If you decide to preach socialism to the general community,
turn to page 78.

If you think that socialism is not the proper goal
and decide to join a social welfare organization, helping the poor,
turn to page 67.

50

You are angry. Don't people understand how terribly oppressed they are? They must be blind to their own situation, to what is wrong in the world. Why should some people have all the money and power? Shouldn't it be shared equally? You've got to take stronger action, do something which will wake people up to the reality.

There are two paths you might follow: one leads toward radical public demonstrations; the other to violent rebellion, to the destruction of society and government, and the rebuilding of an ideal world on the ruins of the old, bad one.

If you decide to organize demonstrations,
turn to page 74.

If rebellion is your choice,
turn to page 75.

51

When your children clean out your office, they find a folder containing stock certificates you had never before mentioned. "Probably another fly-by-night investment," your oldest son says, predicting that the stock will never be worth any money. "But let's keep them anyway. Later, we'll laugh and remember all this trouble; then, it won't seem so bad!"

Your children insist you follow doctor's orders, and the subject of bad judgment is dropped. "Even if you made mistakes and were not always very wise," they say, "parents are still parents, and we love you."

Twenty-five years later, your stock certificates are worth a lot of money. Your children are assured of having a very comfortable future.

END

52

An aged gentleman finds you and nurses you back to health. "We, Arabs, are taught to be like *Ibrahim,* who offered hospitality to his guests. It would be wrong not to help you," he remarks.

After long, slow weeks of recovery, you thank the old man and resume your journey. Finally, you reach your destination. Like generations of pilgrims before you, you kneel down and kiss the soil of the *Holy Land.* Then, you seek out *Rishon Letzion,* the *kibbutz* with which you had made arrangements.

Contented, you work in the vineyards. The grapes you grow are pressed into wine for export to the United States. Probably some of your friends at the farm in Woodbine will drink your wine at their *Pesach seder.* It is a good feeling to know that you are still connected to them.

END

53

The clinic is located on Ninth Avenue, in the heart of what is known as "Little Italy." Most of your patients are Italian, although you do see a smattering of Jewish longshoremen from the Hudson River docks and warehouses. Hard working and honest, these people appreciate what you do for them. They cannot pay you much, but they always pay whatever they promise.

They also pay you with a different king of coin, the coin of respect. When you walk down the street, everyone knows you. "Honored Doctor," they call out, and you feel genuinely honored. Throughout your long medical career, you never have any regrets. You have practiced your chosen profession among people you care for and, in return, they love and respect you. What more could anyone want?

END

54

The area of Prospect Park is one of the nicest areas of Brooklyn. Many of the people who move into its large apartment buildings and handsome, brownstone houses started on the Lower East Side. Most join *Union Temple* or *Beth Elohim,* two *Reform Jewish* congregations more suitable to their new outlook on life.

But these people are not without their problems. Though enjoying the fruits of their success, many still feel attached to their immigrant roots. Their children, however, feel one hundred percent American and reject some of their parents' old ways. Conflicts develop.

You decide to specialize in psychoanalysis, a new branch of medicine developed by *Dr. Sigmund Freud* that helps people lead more satisfied and comfortable lives.

When you become very affluent, you want to perform some *mitzvah* which you believe will make you feel fulfilled. You could offer psychiatric services for free to poor people, or you could help *Rabbi Stephen S. Wise* found a new rabbinical academy.

*If you give free medical help,
turn to page 55.*

*If you prefer to help start the new school,
turn to page 56.*

55

Each morning, you rise at five o'clock and get to your office by six. For three hours, you see patients who cannot afford your services. Their problems are just as real as those of your wealthy clients, and they deserve equal treatment. Your sense of satisfaction grows every day, and their thanks mean more to you than any other payment. You continue treating poor people in this way throughout your career, and when you retire you look back on years of satisfaction and success.

END

56

Rabbi Stephen S. Wise wants to found the *Jewish Institute of Religion,* a school to train liberal rabbis for America. One such rabbinic college, the Hebrew Union College, has existed in Cincinnati, Ohio, since 1875, but *Wise* believes that another is needed in New York and that it must be more open to *Zionism,* tradition, and Hebrew.

You agree and, together with many others, you work tirelessly to raise funds and hire faculty. It is the proudest day in your life when you, once a poor immigrant, march down the aisle of *Temple Emanu-El* and join the graduating class of rabbis being ordained. "I may have left a great deal behind in Europe," you think to yourself, "but I'll never abandon being Jewish."

E N D

57

Now that you've taken the position with the *American Civil Liberties Union* and you remember your cousin who was unable to get a job teaching philosophy because he was Jewish, you are determined to spend your professional life protecting constitutional rights. After all, if a society denies full rights to minorities, then the rights of everyone are endangered.

As you sit at your desk, you remember the *Yekum Purkan,* the prayer of the *siddur,* which has reminded Jews for centuries to pray for the welfare of the country in which they live. The more healthy and free the society, the better life is for all its citizens. You decide to have that prayer mounted on your wall so that you will always remember it.

END

58

You enter the law office with great fear. The new suit that you bought for the interview suddenly doesn't seem to fit. You sit in a big leather chair and stare at the dark wood paneling of the reception room.

Eventually, a secretary leads you to the office of *Louis Marshall,* one of the most famous lawyers of your day. He stands to greet you and asks you to sit down. Within a few moments, you begin to relax, and soon you are talking easily about the law and what you would like to accomplish in the profession. An hour later, *Mr. Marshall* thanks you for coming and tells you that someone from the firm will contact you soon. You thank him for his interest and leave, uncertain whether you should be optimistic or pessimistic about your chances.

*If you are not hired for the job,
but you accept the decision gracefully,
turn to page 61.*

*If you are not hired and become very angry,
turn to page 62.*

*If you get the position,
turn to page 63.*

59

With the profits you have accumulated, you buy several other stores along Orchard Street. One is for ladies' clothing; another for shoes; the third is a small restaurant. You hire a manager for each one, but they all belong to your company: LES Enterprises (Lower East Side Enterprises).

One day, eight of your employees ask to meet with you. "We've worked for you for two years," their representative says, "and we're not satisfied with our pay or working conditions. We have formed a union of all LES Enterprises employees. Either you bargain with us or we strike."

You are surprised. You had thought all of them were happy. Now, you see that you were mistaken. But a union and a strike could pose real problems, especially since you have borrowed a lot of money to buy these stores.

*If you refuse to recognize the union
and decide to take your chances with a strike,
turn to page 65.*

*If you refuse to recognize the union
and decide to sell the business,
turn to page 66.*

60

You decide, however, that expanding on the Lower East Side would not be sensible. Your children are of the same opinion. They remark: "As soon as people get a little bit rich, they move. Those who have money to spend don't live in this area. Let's find a new place where your business can do better."

So you plan to move to one of the suburbs, where you can build a bigger and better business. For six months, you travel around New York and New Jersey, looking for a promising business opportunity. Finally, you narrow the choice down to three possibilities.

If you decide to go to Brooklyn,
turn to page 95.

If the Bronx attracts you,
turn to page 96.

If you set up a business in Hoboken, New Jersey,
turn to page 97.

61

*M*r. *Marshall*'s letter explains that you simply would not fit into the firm. "You come from a very different culture," he writes, and you realize that it was probably too much to expect that an *Eastern European* Jewish lawyer could be part of a *German-Jewish* law firm.

"Maybe I had better stay where I belong," you think. You return to the Lower East Side. Your law practice there is moderately successful, and you feel satisfaction as you help your fellow new-Americans with their legal concerns.

As you look back, you conclude that everything has turned out for the best. You have done important work among people you care about.

E N D

62

Louis Marshall's letter implies that you did not get the job because you are not trained in the area of law in which they specialize. You are furious because you know you are qualified for the job. It must be that *Marshall* is prejudiced against *Eastern European Jews.* "I did not drag myself out of the Lower East Side and through law school just to have some *uptown German Jew* spit on me. If that's what being a Jew means, I want no part of it!" You are determined that you will never lose another opportunity just because you are Jewish.

You walk across Central Park in Manhattan and enter *Dr. Felix Adler*'s *Society for Ethical Culture.* You've heard that it retains the best of Judaism without the ceremonies and without the social disadvantages—but also without having to become Christian.

You become a prominent attorney in New York. When you have reached a ripe old age, you retire. But you will always wonder if what you rejected in Judaism did not really mean more than you want to admit.

E N D

63

Full of pride and determination, you begin your new job in *Louis Marshall*'s law firm. You are one of the first Lower East Siders to move *uptown,* and you want to prove that you are worthy of the opportunity. You work very hard, two years go by, and, although you know that you've done well, no one tells you so.

The very next pay day, however, when you open your monthly pay envelope, the check is much larger than the previous month. You are sure that there has been a mistake. Carrying the check, you knock on *Mr. Marshall*'s office door. When you enter, before you have a chance to say anything, he holds up his hand and tells you. "I have a little surprise for you. You've done so well here that we have just promoted you to junior partner. Congratulations!"

A huge smile breaks across your face. You've been accepted, and you're on the road to success!

END

64

When you become a rabbi, you decide to move back to the Lower East Side. Rather than take a congregational pulpit, you accept a position at the *Henry Street Settlement House.* Together with its director, *Lillian Wald,* you help immigrant Jews and others find housing, food, clothing, fuel, and jobs. You teach them English and advise them how to manage in this new country.

Somehow, the *socialism* of your youth gets left behind. You are content to do *mitzvot* among these people, to help them achieve their own goals. You may not have changed all of society, but you certainly have helped a lot of people, and that makes you very happy.

END

65

The workers, bitterly angry, walk off the job, putting up picket lines in front of each store and blocking each entrance. This has never happened before. LES Enterprises and you have become a test case in the power of unions.

Late night rallies are held by the workers. *Meyer London* speaks to them about *socialism* and the need for collective action. Even though the strike is difficult for them and their families, they persist.

You are sympathetic to their needs. After all, it was not so long ago that you, too, were a peddler. You know that it is difficult to raise a family on what your workers earn. But you also know that your business would probably fail if you raised their wages. Then everyone would suffer.

It dawns on you that the *bet din* has helped solve many problems. Maybe they can show you the right way.

*If you turn to the rabbinical bet din
and ask them to resolve the controversy,
turn to page 93.*

*If you decide to work things out for yourself,
turn to page 94.*

66

The workers go on strike, and you realize that this cannot continue. It would mean your ruin and your return to peddling. But you cannot bring yourself to recognize the union. After all the bitterness of the strike, the names they have called you, the insults and the difficulties, it would be just too much for you to give in and admit defeat.

But, you have also lost interest in running the business. Your heart is just not in the effort anymore.

One day, while you are having a glass of tea at the corner cafe, you get an idea. Why not sell the business to the employees? Then, you will be rid of it, and they can manage it anyway they want. You can also pay back the money you borrowed and make a nice profit.

You call a meeting with a delegation of workers and present your offer. They ask for time to think it over. After twenty-four hours, they come back, agree to the terms, and you work out the sale quickly. Everyone seems happy. You can retire now comfortably, and they have control over the amount of money they will earn and the conditions under which they will work. One of the workers leans over to you after the sale is completed and says: "You're not so bad after all. This deal is worthy of *Solomon.*"

E N D

67

"My family always lived in *Kapulia*," you remember. Just down the street from where you live is a building which houses the *Kapulyer Farband,* where all your Old Country friends meet to help each other. Every week, each member contributes a little money to the treasury so that when one of them becomes ill, or has a special need, or a family member dies, financial help is always available. This *landsmannschaft,* as such mutual aid societies are called, is supported and run by its members. Its work is important to the community. You become an active member. The others have confidence in you, and soon you run the office. The pay is meager, but the rewards are great, and you have the satisfaction that your work really makes a difference.

E N D

68

It seems that your choice was not so bad. Most of the *kosher* butchers chose to move; now only you and one other shop remain on the Lower East Side. More and more customers know your reputation for honesty and buy meat from you. You buy out your partner who wants to move. No longer do you worry about paying your bills and providing for your family's welfare.

One day, the president of the *shul* in which you *daven* comes into your shop, takes you aside, and asks you to serve on the synagogue's board of trustees. You accept and rush home. You exclaim to your family: "Look at me! Suddenly, I'm a *ganze macher!*"

Although you still live in the same small apartment, you are now able to send one son to *City College of New York*. The other son elects to join you in the business. Your daughter has become a secretary. As they begin their own families, your children move out to new housing developments on Long Island. Every *Pesach*, your children and grandchildren gather in your apartment for the *seder*. As they do, you recline in your chair and thank God that you and your family have been blessed in so many ways.

END

69

Moving to *Harlem* required a great deal of serious thinking; it was not easy to leave the old neighborhood where you still had a few friends. But you've made up your mind, and your partner buys you out.

Your new shop is located *uptown* on 125th Street, a wide, tree-lined avenue that is always filled with people. You see your old friends and make new ones. Your children attend a good public school.

There is only one problem: When the Jews in your new neighborhood pass your store, they don't enter. It seems that many of them left their traditional practices back on the Lower East Side. Many no longer keep *kosher,* especially when non-*kosher* meat a block away is so much cheaper than yours.

After six months of struggling to stay in business, you realize that the move was a mistake. You decide to sell the shop and return to the Lower East Side.

E N D

70

After several years of preparatory studies, you are admitted to the rabbinical department at JTS. You have been supported by a scholarship from the *Warburg* family, so you are determined to do well in your studies—and you do! You find the long hours learning *Talmud* interesting and feel at home with the Seminary's combination of modern thought and traditional practice.

Just before you are ordained as a rabbi, the placement director tells you of two special opportunities. You could go back to the Lower East Side and work with immigrants at the *Educational Alliance.* As another option, you could become a military chaplain and work to relieve the misery of European Jews caused by *World War I.*

If you decide to return to your old neighborhood,
turn to page 86.

If you prefer the overseas assignment,
turn to page 87.

71

You stride into the fight, swinging a baseball bat, scaring the thugs away. They had not expected you and your friends to fight with such determination. The owner finally realizes that it would be best for everyone to settle the strike.

As your friends congratulate you, a man in a business suit hands you his card. It says that he is a scout from the New York Yankees. "I saw you swing that bat," he says. "You're pretty good. How about trying out for the team?"

You don't know much about baseball, but why not? It's easier than sewing on a machine and more fun than hitting a thug with a bat. You are an instant success. You can hit the ball very well. Soon, you are one of the stars. Your future is assured.

END

72

You hold up a white flag and cross the street. The leader of the gang comes out to meet you. "Listen," you say, "you know what is going to happen. Some of us will get hurt and so will some of you. Who benefits? Not us and not you, but the owner. Why should we spill each other's blood for an owner who wouldn't fight for us?"

Everyone thinks for a moment and then agrees. It's not worth a fight. The only one who will win is the owner. Instead of battling an enemy, you make new friends.

When the owner sees that bullying you doesn't help, the only reasonable thing is to settle the strike. It was a wise decision. You are elected president of the new union; everyone respects your good judgment.

END

73

Your campaign as a reformer against *Tammany Hall* challenges the political bosses. They send a gang of toughs to beat you up, but anticipating their tactics you protected yourself with bodyguards. The more the bosses threaten you, the greater your determination to throw them out of office. *Tammany Hall*'s power must be broken.

When the votes are in, the residents of the Lower East Side have elected you their representative. You are very proud and promise to do your best. But they are so accustomed to paying bribes to city officials that many people now come to you with envelopes full of money or boxes full of merchandise. You know that in exchange for these gifts one day they'll want favors or help.

If you decide to refuse their bribes,
turn to page 91.

If you decide that such gifts are a normal part
of politics and you pocket the bribes,
turn to page 92.

74

With *Emma Goldman* and other friends who think as you do, you begin to organize a huge demonstration for *May 1.* You will hold a banner saying, *"Workers of the world, unite,"* and everyone will sing the *Marseillaise.*

On the day of the demonstration, a huge crowd gathers at the corner of Canal Street and East Broadway for the march to *City Hall.*

But the route is blocked by hundreds of police armed with clubs. They are as determined to prevent you from reaching *City Hall* as you are to carry through with the demonstration. There can be no compromise. Suddenly, police on horseback charge down upon you. You try to fight back, but they club you down and haul you off to jail with scores of other demonstrators. You are sentenced to a long jail term for inciting to riot. It will be a long time before you have to make your next life choice.

E N D

75

Society and government are corrupt, you decide. All power seems to lie in the hands of evil people, while good citizens suffer. The only remedy is to destroy the present society so that it can be rebuilt in an ethical and moral fashion.

You and a few close associates decide that the way to start the revolution is to assassinate several leading politicians and business magnates. You are put in charge of manufacturing the bombs that will accomplish this goal.

Unknown to you, however, one of your group is a spy for the *FBI*. One night, just before you are ready to bomb the mayor's office, police raid your headquarters and arrest you. You are convicted of conspiring to commit murder. Rather than send you to jail, the government decides to deport you. You are sent back to Russia, never to be allowed to return to America.

E N D

76

Carrots grow well in southern New Jersey. You work hard and get great satisfaction as the long rows of feathery green tops rise above the soil. An expert from the *National Farm School* comes out to advise you on improving the crop, and his plan works. Your carrot crop is a huge success.

When you count up the profits, you realize that you have made a substantial sum. You decide that some of the money should be used for *tsedakah.* You make contributions to the *National Farm School* and to the *Hebrew Immigrant Aid Society.* After all, you should not be the only one to benefit from *David Lubin*'s good advice.

With the rest of the money, you buy a bigger farm and grow more carrots. You know now your future is here, on this farm. You marry and start a family. Life is good to you. Your future and that of your children are now secure.

E N D

77

The red cabbage grows nicely. After the harvest, you truck your crop into New York City and set up a stand to sell it.

You read in the newspaper that everyone is excited about the *Bolsheviks* in Russia. Many think they are a great threat, but some of the Jews on the Lower East Side are sympathetic to the "Red" or *Communist Revolution.* You, however, think they are mistaken.

Suddenly, a mob comes around the corner. They are looking to beat up Jewish "Reds." They see your stand of red cabbage and rush toward you. "It's just like those Jews. They aren't content to think treacherous thoughts. They even sell 'red' vegetables."

They turn your stand over, set fire to it, and beat you bloody. After they leave, you stagger to the home of friends. You are ruined and must start all over again. You are very disillusioned and bitter.

Turn to page 26.

78

To reach the general community, you must go where they live . . . and that's *uptown*. With the *Socialist party*'s help, you open an office on Madison Avenue and begin to publish a monthly newsletter. Your campaign to gain greater acceptance for *Socialist* ideas is somewhat successful.

But as you reflect on your achievement you realize that, if you can sell *socialism,* you can sell anything. Advertising seems to be the key to the modern world, so you enter the advertising business. You abandon *socialism* as you try to convince people to buy various products.

You are very successful and make a great deal of money. The prestige of your ad agency grows, and soon many people work for you.

One day, you meet an old friend from the Lower East Side. "Aha," he exclaims. "Now, look at you. A big capitalist. Is that what comes from trying to teach *socialism?* Bah!" After he leaves, you think to yourself. "Am I a sell-out? Maybe. But then maybe I'm just not really a *Socialist.* Now, at last, I am happy. Isn't it OK to change one's mind? Isn't it part of growing up?"

E N D

79

You sail for France on a magnificent ocean liner, far different from the overcrowded and smelly ship you took when you first crossed the Atlantic. Even the third-class cabin that you booked has every comfort you need. You have a very enjoyable trip.

Before long, you arrive at the port of Le Havre along with hundreds of other people making *aliyah,* like you. You cross Europe by train, arrive at Salonika, a Greek port, then Constantinople on the European part of Turkey. From there you board a small boat to cross the Bosporus and find yourself in the Asian part of Turkey.

You travel the rest of your journey by train once again across Turkey, Syria, Lebanon and finally you arrive in Palestine. You kiss the soil and your first desire is to visit the *Western Wall* like thousands of your ancestors had done before you. It is a dream come true!

END

80

Your ship lands in Naples, a beautiful city. You would like to spend a few days sightseeing, especially in the ruins of Pompeii, but you are so anxious to get to Palestine that you board another ship for the Turkish port of Izmir in Asia Minor.

Now, the difficult part of the journey begins. You hire a guide and a mule and set out to cross Turkey, Syria, and Lebanon on your way to Palestine. You have been told that the Turkish authorities do not want any more Jews to move into the country and that they have given their permission to brigands to bar the way and even to attack Jewish travelers. You're willing to risk the danger, however, because getting to Palestine is your most important goal.

Just as you approach the city of Latakia in Syria, a band of robbers assaults you. They do not harm your guide because he has purposely led you right into their trap. They take your money and beat you unconscious. They leave, expecting you to die.

Turn to page 52.

81

You store the whalebone in a warehouse, waiting for just the right moment. The following week, you read in *The New York Times* that a huge storm has struck the whaling fleet. About half the ships and many men have been lost. You knew some of those people, and you sit in your office mourning them. You plan to visit their families to pay your condolences.

Ironically, their disaster is your fortune. The shortage of whalebone makes your warehouse supply very valuable. Other manufacturers, in need of the whalebone, bid higher and higher. You finally get a very good price. The gamble paid off. You are now very wealthy and live the rest of your life in comfort. You also have money to give to the widows of the whalers and lots of spare time to spend as a leader in charitable organizations. As you near the end of your days, you feel that your life has been worthwhile.

END

82

Shortly after you buy all the whalebone, a chemical company announces that they have invented a new substance—plastic. All the other corset makers switch from whalebone to stays of the new material. It is just as strong and lasts as long as whalebone, but it is much cheaper. Your corsets are now more expensive than those made by your competitors.

You had bought more than enough for your immediate needs, wanting to have a whole year's supply of corset stays. Now, you're stuck with the big investment in whalebone, and you must try to get rid of it. You manage to sell some to the *Smithsonian Institution* for scientific research, but you're forced to use the rest for your corsets, even though it means selling them at a loss.

You go broke; all your dreams of riches fail to come true. Your only alternative now is to spend the rest of your life working for someone else.

END

83

The major influence in your studies is *Morris Raphael Cohen,* a brilliant teacher of modern philosophy. You study hard and earn your Ph.D. degree.

You apply for teaching positions at many colleges and are well recommended by the faculty, but you receive rejection after rejection.

Finally, you discover through a friend at *Columbia University* that colleges do not want to hire Jewish teachers. You decide to fight their prejudice. You hire an attorney and inform the dean of Columbia that you will sue unless the faculty's biased decision is reversed.

Two weeks later, you are told that a position as instructor is available. You accept the job. It's not the best paid or most exciting teaching post in the world, but it is a start.

END

84

When you graduate from *City College of New York,* you are accepted into medical school at *New York University.* You have never worked so hard in your life. At one point in your studies, you almost give up and quit. But that day at *Shacharit* you recite a prayer in which God is described as a *Faithful and Merciful Healer.* You realize that curing people of disease is a very special gift and decide to persist and obtain your medical degree.

Finally, the great day comes. Your Cousin Hyman is your only relative in America, and he is there, cheering as you become a doctor. You wish with all your heart that your parents could see you, so you have a photographer take your picture. At least they'll be able to see how you looked on this happy day.

There are two positions open to you. A doctor is urgently needed in a clinic for workers in an industrial part of the city. On the other hand, the residential area of Prospect Park in Brooklyn could use a physician.

If you join the clinic,
turn to page 53.

If you open a practice in Prospect Park,
turn to page 54.

85

Your legal studies give you great satisfaction. You enjoy the intellectual challenge, and arguing cases in "mock court" is one of the high points of every week. As you travel back and forth between your small apartment and the law school, you are always reading. People on the streetcar begin to refer to you as "The Judge."

Finally, you graduate law school with high honors. Many jobs are open to you, but two have special appeal. The *American Civil Liberties Union* (ACLU) offers you a position defending the civil rights of people who have been treated unfairly. A big *uptown* law firm also bids for your services, and you are given a date for an interview. Should you be hired, you would be the first *Eastern European* Jewish lawyer to join such a firm.

If you accept the ACLU position,
turn to page 57.

If you opt for the interview,
turn to page 58.

86

Back on the Lower East Side, you devote your life to helping teenage Jewish immigrants adjust to America. You organize English language classes and find ways for them to learn various trades and occupations. On Sundays, you and the young people often board streetcars and go on picnics in Central Park in Manhattan or on excursions to Coney Island in Brooklyn. After work, you and some of your young friends sometimes attend lectures at the *Cooper Union,* where you listen to some of the great speakers of the time, such as *Stephen S. Wise, David Dubinsky, Samuel Gompers,* and *Morris Raphael Cohen.*

You also try to teach them that it is possible to live as a religious Jew in America. A few changes must be made in the ancient traditions, but the fundamentals need not be lost. You teach the young people that they can still be faithful sons and daughters of the covenant that was first given at Sinai.

Many decades later you retire with a deep sense of satisfaction. You have assisted many people and helped preserve Judaism in America. In a surprise tribute to you, the *Jewish Theological Seminary* awards you an honorary doctoral degree. You sit down after the presentation and pray: "Lord, I know that my people appreciate what I have tried to do; may my life also be acceptable to You. Amen."

END

87

You enlist as an army chaplain while *World War I* is raging throughout Europe. Particularly devastated are the Jews of Eastern Europe who live in the *Pale of Settlement*. The warring armies of eastern and western Europe have crisscrossed the Pale, destroying villages and farms, forcing thousands to flee their homes without food or proper clothing. Hundreds of thousands of Jewish refugees desperately need help, so you arrange to transfer to the *Joint Distribution Committee* (JDC).

People from more tranquil Jewish communities have contributed a great deal of money to the JDC. You and other workers spend these funds helping people resettle and start their lives over again. The work is so satisfying that you make a career of working for the JDC.

As you retire and reflect on your life, you remember your own beginnings as a poor immigrant. You decide that you have come a long way and that you have been extremely fortunate. The chance that Cousin Hyman once gave you, you have now been able to pass on to thousands of others.

END

88

You round up some of your strongest and biggest friends and plan for a real battle. The thugs are standing at the corner of Allen and Grand streets in the Lower East Side, and you decide to face them. You and your group head in that direction.

When you turn the corner onto Allen Street, you have second thoughts. Is it really necessary to fight? Besides, the thugs look pretty strong; they are armed with thick bats and other fearsome weapons.

If you decide that fight is the only solution, turn to page 71.

If you decide to talk sense with the toughs, turn to page 72.

89

The focus of your efforts is the *Cooper Union,* where people come at night and on weekends to hear lectures. You believe that you can reach those people and influence them to fight for *socialism.*

While you are preaching your ideas, you are overheard by *Rabbi Stephen S. Wise.* He approaches you, introduces himself, and tells you that he likes what you have said. Many of the ideas you propose were first proposed by the prophets of the Bible, he tells you to your great surprise. Sharing all resources equally, concern for the poor, and demanding justice for all are ancient Jewish ideas. He suggests that you would be a good rabbi and offers to sponsor you in his school, the *Jewish Institute of Religion.*

You accept his offer and, after several years of rabbinic training, are ordained as a rabbi.

Turn to page 64.

90

As head of the "Commercial Division," you discover that *Tammany Hall* has told hundreds of store owners that they must pay monthly "protection" money if they want to remain in business. If they refuse to pay, it's your job to see that a gang of thugs beats them up or sets fire to their stores. Since you are making so much more money illegally than you could legally, you do whatever you are told and close your eyes to the violence and crime you and your bosses commit. You are sure you have nothing to worry about because *Tammany Hall* has bribed the police to leave you alone.

When the reform ticket wins the next election, however, a new police commissioner, *Theodore A. Bingham,* is appointed. He is especially interested in Jewish criminals, so much so that many believe he is an anti-Semite. After all, most of the guilty people of *Tammany Hall* are not Jews, but he seems to concentrate only on Jews.

One day, as you reach your office, you and dozens of others are arrested. You are convicted in court for arson, assault, and theft and are sentenced to life imprisonment. You spend the rest of your days in the penitentiary.

END

91

In the *cheder,* back in the Old Country, you were taught: "Lord, who may dwell in Your house? . . . He who does not take a bribe against innocent people." (Psalm 15:1,5) You remember this verse and know that it is as true today as when *David* wrote it. You know that honesty will always guide you in your decisions.

People from all walks of life come to you, knowing that you are honest and are willing to help those in need. You are reelected many times and finally retire as an honored person in your community. At your retirement ceremony, the mayor reads a proclamation stating that you have always worn *"the crown of a good name."*

A few days later, you receive a call from Washington, D.C. The country needs your help: millions are unemployed as a result of a terrible economic depression. Your reputation has reached the nation's capital where the president wants you to organize a new program of public relief. You are honored to accept.

As you ride the train, you reflect back. You've come a long way from poor immigrant to presidential advisor. You are proud that you did so without being unfaithful to the Jewish ideals you were taught. As you lean back you recite the traditional *Shehecheyanu:* "Praised are You, O Lord our God, Ruler of the universe, for giving us life, for sustaining us, and for enabling us to reach this day. Amen."

END

92

What began by taking just a few "presents" turned into a career of political corruption. You're doing now what you started fighting against when you left *Tammany Hall*. But, eventually, it catches up with you. One of your assistants rushes in to tell you that, by bribing a clerk at precinct headquarters, he learned the police are coming to arrest you.

You cannot allow your family to be disgraced by such a scandal. You decide to get rid of all incriminating evidence by setting fire to a wastebasket filled with the papers recording all your corrupt activities. Now, without proof, you cannot be convicted. But your name and reputation have been tarnished, anyway, and you decide to leave the Lower East Side. All of your good future is lost; nothing can ever be the same.

E N D

93

The two *dayanim* sit beside the *av bet din* as the rabbinical court hears first one side, then the other. Both you and your workers testify about the problems at work and the difficulty of reaching a fair solution. Finally, the three judges leave the room. You know they are searching through the books of Jewish law to reach a fair decision.

When they return, you are very nervous. The chief judge begins: "The holy *Torah* instructs us in this case, 'You shall certainly open your hand to him [the poor person], lending him enough to satisfy his needs.' (Deuteronomy 15:8) From this verse, we learn that the store owner must grant the demands of the workers: they must be able to earn enough money on which to live. But 'to satisfy his needs' also applies to the owner's needs. We cannot force the owner into bankruptcy. Therefore, the demands will be granted over a three-year period, one-third each year. That way, everyone will shoulder a fair share of the burden."

You and the workers are equally satisfied. As all of you leave the *bet din* together, you agree: "It's a good thing we worked this dispute out in a Jewish court. Now, we can still be friends and work together. *Baruch Hashem,* praised be God for giving us a law that helps us manage our quarrels among ourselves in dignity and peace."

E N D

94

You call another meeting with the representatives of the workers. The bargaining session is stormy and tense. People yell at each other and pound on the table. No agreement seems possible, so you stand up and leave. As you walk out of the building, an angry crowd of workers hurls insults at you. A tomato splatters against your coat, and a rotten egg barely misses your head. Frightened and trembling, you walk quickly home, taunted by the mob.

As you slump into a chair, you feel a sharp pain in your chest and down your left arm. You scream to your family: "Call the doctor!" But it's too late. The heart attack is massive, and you die.

Trying to hold out was of no use; now, everything has been lost.

END

95

The East River separates Brooklyn from Manhattan, so you cross the Brooklyn Bridge and settle in the Flatbush section of Brooklyn. You buy a nice house on a nice street with a single tree growing outside your house. But, now, after spending more than you expected on the house, you find yourself without enough money to begin the big business you had in mind.

You consider something small in the Coney Island area because you noticed during your six-months' research that there were very few restaurants or food stands there. Quickly-prepared and inexpensive food is especially hard to find. You open a small food stand and sell simple things, like good hot dogs, cold drinks, and ices. In memory of your father who died in Europe after you left home, you name the stand after him: Nathan's. It becomes a huge success. Your future is secure.

END

96

You arrive in the Bronx, north of Manhattan, and enjoy fields and forests which were one of the reasons for your choice. It's like being out in the country. It feels so good! The Grand Concourse is a wide, airy, quiet avenue, lined with tall shade trees and handsome apartment houses. It certainly wasn't like this on the Lower East Side.

Finding the right location for the right business is harder than you expected. But you're not sorry you made the Bronx your choice. You take a job driving a truck for the City of New York. The pay is less than what you might have made from your own business, but you feel more secure. Once hired, you cannot be fired easily.

Your bank account continues to grow, although at a slower pace. Before long, however, you can afford to buy a small home and a car. You have a comfortable and pleasant life. You play cards every Saturday afternoon with a group of Jewish neighbors and on Sundays you spend the day out, enjoying nature. Although you no longer go to the synagogue, you do have a *mezuzah* on your door and you perform *mitzvot.*

E N D

97

Y ou move to Hoboken, in New Jersey, where you open a small factory. It's hard work. Sometimes the union calls a strike, and the factory is shut down for a short while. But you are a reasonable boss and you do not want to hurt your workers or yourself. So the strikes are usually settled very quickly, and you do not suffer any bad consequences.

Because your workers respect you as a fair employer, they are more productive. A happy worker always makes a better worker. You also show that you care about their families, and on *Chanukah* you send them gifts.

You grow old, loved and honored by everyone. When you die, all the workers collect money to plant a grove of trees in Palestine in your memory.

E N D

98

You accept the terms your workers propose, and your business begins to operate at a profit, even with the added costs of the strike settlement. You are able to make up some of those new expenses by raising your prices. In addition, your satisfied workers are more productive. You know you did the right thing in agreeing to settle the strike and meet your workers' demands, especially because both you and your workers could continue to observe Shabbat. Preserving the traditional practice allowed everyone a sense of dignity, and you conclude that this self-respect is far more valuable and important than anything money could ever buy.

END

99

You reject the terms offered by the union and expect the strike to be a long one. The future doesn't look very good. Things around you, in the outside world, aren't very good either. Europe is at war; the United States has just entered the war, too. The Army will need many uniforms, and you decide to lobby in Washington for a government contract. You make the trip, taking home a big order, which permits you to meet the union's demands and settle the strike.

The demand for uniforms increases. You hire more workers and pay them extra to work longer hours. The War Department awards you a certificate of honor for producing the uniforms quickly. You are proud of your entire factory.

Turn to page 106.

100

Late at night, you and your family pack a few belongings in a suitcase. You sneak a look out the window. A big surprise greets you. Word of your plan to escape has leaked out. Workers are surrounding your home, arm-in-arm. You cannot escape through their human chain.

Your children begin to cry. The pressure of the strike seems too much for all of you. You realize that holding out longer will be destructive for everyone, and you ask for another meeting with the union committee. At that meeting, you settle the strike.

Later, you decide to sell the business. Your heart is no longer in it. You take the money from the sale, move away, and are never heard from again.

E N D

101

You call the police and explain the situation. They send a squad of men who quickly clear away the pickets. The sergeant comes up to you and tells you that the way is now clear. He also tells you: "Always glad to help. These Jews are always causing trouble. Nothing but riff-raff. We need to show them who's boss."

This open display of anti-Semitism shocks you. You thought that this kind of feeling only existed in Europe. Obviously, you were mistaken. You feel you must do something about it.

If you meet with other Jewish owners
to organize a common response,
turn to page 107.

If you choose to close your business and move away,
turn to page 108.

102

Everyone goes back to work, but the union leadership starts to plan, preparing for any future strike. Food, clothing, blankets, coal, and other necessities are collected and stored so that they can be distributed to the workers and their families as needed. Every week, each worker pays a little money into a newly-established strike fund. Even if the strike lasts a long time, there will be enough money to help buy what people need. You will never let the union members who depend on you be caught unprepared again. Being a leader, you realize, involves a lot of responsibility.

E N D

103

You run from the fight, but you feel cowardly and know that you have disgraced youself in public. You sit down on a bench in Seward Park in the Lower East Side, really depressed, and think about the whole situation. There must be another way; standing your ground and fighting doesn't solve anything. Then, you have a brainstorm.

You go to the local bank and talk with the manager. Your boss has borrowed a good deal of money from the bank, and the payments of those loans depend on the settlement of the strike. If the owner does not give in, the money cannot be repaid, and the bank might demand to be paid immediately.

In fact, the bank cannot afford to lose such a sum of money, and the owner is requested to pay without delay. The owner has no choice but to settle the strike. When word of how the settlement was reached gets out, you are acclaimed as a hero. You continue through life as a well-respected person.

E N D

104

You agree to buy Mr. Levi's delicatessen from his widow. The store is located on Delancey Street near Essex Street, an area always crowded with people from dawn to dusk. You are convinced you can turn the shop into a thriving business. With some friends, you spend many hours refurbishing the interior, cleaning the floor, the walls, the furniture, making your new restaurant sparkle.

You realize that you must decide what kind of food you will serve, what kind of customers you wish to attract. There are many *Yiddish*-speaking intellectuals on the Lower East Side who do not care if the food is *kosher* or not. On the other hand, you also know that a *kosher* restaurant serving only *milchiks* would be popular.

If you open a cafe for Yiddish-speaking intellectuals, turn to page 113.

If you open a kosher restaurant, turn to page 109.

105

An interview is arranged with the Police Department through a friend of your uncle, Yankel. You understand that a "present" has to be sent to the captain of the precinct. It doesn't sound quite right, but that's the way things are done.

Captain O'Reilly interviews you. He asks you many questions and then gives you a test to see how strong you are. You pass, and he recommends you enroll in the new class of recruits.

After you graduate from the police academy, you are offered two assignments.

If you decide to become a horse-patrol officer, turn to page 110.

If you choose to become a detective, turn to page 111.

106

After the war, you expect to return to a quieter and more peaceful life. But it doesn't happen that way. Most of your European relatives still live in the *Pale of Settlement* in Russia. During the war, this area had been one of the main battlegrounds. One army after another had marched across the Pale, taking its food, destroying its buildings, and devastating both agriculture and business. Life for the millions of Jews in this region has been totally disrupted, and many are dying of starvation and disease.

Your relatives need help. They have written to you asking for boat tickets to America, and you feel you must help them. After all, that's what a *mishpachah* is for. You devote every penny you made to resettling your relatives. You give them jobs in your business. It was difficult, but you feel good about it. Taking care of one's own is the most basic form of *tsedakah*.

END

107

The other Jewish business owners have similar tales to tell. Your experience is not unique. All agree that an organization to protect Jewish rights is needed. But you cannot do it by yourselves. The wealthy and influential Jews *uptown* are needed as well.

With their help, the *Kehillah* is organized. Together, you feel much stronger and more able to respond to anti-Semitism.

However, the *Kehillah* moves far beyond the question of anti-Semitism. It works to improve conditions of life and work for New York Jews, helps them educate themselves to become better Americans, and performs many other important functions.

Having had a part in the organization of such a valuable group, you realize how unfair you had been to your workers and call off the strike. From this time on, you will try to get along with them in a more cooperative way.

E N D

108

You decide that the only possibility is to close the business and move away. The strike has caused such angry feelings that you and the workers will never be able to cooperate again.

The workers are shocked by the news that they have lost their jobs. They never expected the strike to lead to this, and they ask you to reconsider. But you've made up your mind and persist in your decision. You sell your stock and your equipment. One day, a truck pulls up to your home. All your furniture and personal effects are loaded, and you and your family leave. You never return to the Lower East Side again.

E N D

109

People are very excited about your new restaurant. They miss the types of Jewish food they had eaten in Europe and are overjoyed that now there is a place in New York where they can eat what they like. You decide to specialize in *blintzes* and *knishes*—only dairy dishes, since the restaurant is too small to have *two kitchens.*

Business booms. Your family grows. As your eldest daughter reaches the age of eighteen, you ask the *shadchan* to find a suitable young husband for such a fine daughter.

She marries the son of a merchant, and they, in turn, raise a fine family. You love your grandchildren, and you are very proud of your own rise from poverty. You are happy and, as you look back, you realize that America has lived up to your expectations.

END

110

You ride your tall brown horse through the streets. Children follow you everywhere, and you are very proud. The older folks are pleased to see a Jewish person on the police force and name you the "*Yiddishe* cowboy."

One day, you are alerted to a robbery that is taking place a few blocks from your post. You spur your horse to a gallop and dash toward the scene. Just as you come around the corner of Essex Street, an automobile turns onto Houston Street. Your horse, frightened at the sight and sound of the vehicle, throws you under the wheels of the car.

You are seriously injured and can never ride again. The Police Benevolent Association helps you out. You get a pension, and you spend the rest of your life as a semi-invalid. It's not the way you planned your life . . . but you are grateful to be alive. You find also that now you have more time to perform more *mitzvot* than you were able to when you had a full-time job.

As you raise the *Kiddush* cup on *Shabbat,* you greet your family and guests with "Lechayim,"—"To life."

END

111

Being a detective interests you. The cases require much thought. One *Shabbat* afternoon, between *Minchah* and *Ma'ariv,* while you are studying *Talmud* with some friends, you stop reading and break out laughing. The friends call out: "Nu, so what's the joke?" "I finally understand," you reply. "I'm doing just what my ancestors have always done. We use our brains to puzzle out problems. It's just that I'm using a different kind of law!"

You do your job well and are promoted. Five years after you started, you are a lieutenant. The Police Department transfers you to Brooklyn, where you buy a small house near Coney Island. It is a time of great contentment for you—a fine family, a new home, a good job. The future looks very bright, indeed.

END

112

You advise everyone to forget about unions. They might be effective some time in the future, but now is not the time. "Better to earn what we can and take care of our families than to stand up for our ideals and starve."

Things return to normal as everyone goes back to work. As you leave the sweatshop one night, a group of young Jewish workers surround you and yell at you. *"Scab,* strikebreaker, tool of the owners," they call you. "You sold out our future. We were prepared to stay on strike, but you gave in. Coward, fool. . . ."

That night, as you lie in bed, you understand that some things are even more valuable than a full stomach. The young workers are right. You made the wrong decision.

The next day, you pack your bags and move away. You have decided to resign as a union organizer and enroll in college.

Turn to page 42.

113

Your cafe thrives. People are always coming in and out; a crowd of intellectuals sits around the tables, someone is always arguing. Copies of the *Forvarts* and *Tageblatt* are shared back and forth as different people express their points of view. *Abraham Goldfaden* is a frequent visitor, as are other well-known people. You are enchanted by their talk and the hustle-bustle of your place.

One day, your assistant comes up to you and pulls you away from their conversation, saying: "*Nudnick,* don't you see what is happening? All they do is sit there all day with one stale glass of tea. Spend money? They don't even know what that means. Look in the cash box. There is hardly enough to pay the bills."

The intellectual crowd is fun to have around, and you don't listen to your assistant who, of course, is right. Your customers are really *Luftmenschen,* but you cannot eat air. The cafe goes out of business.

While you were waiting on the customers, however, you had listened to the *Socialist* arguments. Some of their ideas sounded interesting, and now you wonder if they might not be right, after all.

Turn to page 10.

Glossary

Adler, Felix (1851–1933) · Reform Jewish rabbi who refused to accept traditional religious Judaism and founded the Society for Ethical Culture.

Adler, Jacob (1855–1926) · Most important figure on the Yiddish stage.

Al Chet · Prayer for the confession of sins recited during the Yom Kippur services. (For *Yom Kippur,* see glossary below.)

Aliyah · Moving from another country to Palestine which, after 1948, became Israel.

Amalgamated Clothing Workers of America · The union of workers in the men's clothing industry; founded in 1914.

American Civil Liberties Union (ACLU) · Founded in 1920, the ACLU worked to defend unpopular causes and persons, including labor unions, political dissenters and radicals, aliens and minority groups, when their constitutional rights were threatened. For many of these people, the ACLU was their only protection.

Av Bet Din · The head of a rabbinical court. (For *Bet Din,* see below.)

Bar Mitzvah · A male Jew who becomes obligated to fulfill the commandments. Also the ceremony for boys at age thirteen which signifies that they are now considered adults by the Jewish religion.

Baruch Hashem · Hebrew phrase meaning "Blessed be The Name" or "Thank God."

Bashert · Yiddish word meaning "predetermined by fate."

Bet Din · Rabbinical court which can decide all cases except criminal matters.

Beth Elohim · Reform Jewish temple in Brooklyn.

Bingham, Theodore A. · Police commissioner of New York City who, in 1908, accused Jews of taking an especially large part in crime. His charges were not true, although some Jews did engage in illegal acts.

Blintzes · Thin pancakes filled with fruit or cheese.

Bolsheviks · Russian revolutionaries who overthrew the tsar's government in 1917. Often called Communists. (See definition below for *Tsar.*)

Brandeis, Louis D. (1856–1941) · Attorney who became a justice of the United States Supreme Court. Also famous as a labor negotiator and leader of American Zionism. (See *Zionism* in glossary.)

Braslau, Sophie · Contralto star of the Metropolitan Opera from 1920 to 1934. Daughter of a Lower East Side doctor.

Cahan, Abraham (1860–1951) · Author, Socialist leader, and editor of the *Forvarts (Jewish Daily Forward),* a Yiddish newspaper in New York, for nearly 50 years.

Chalah · Braided egg bread used for the Sabbath.

Chanukah · Eight-day festival usually in December which celebrates the victory of the Jews over the Seleucids in 165 B.C.E. This was the first war ever fought for freedom of religion.

Chasidim (Singular: Chasid) · Followers of Chasidism, a movement founded by Baal Shem Tov (1699–1761).

Chazan · The cantor, the person who chants the prayers of the religious service.

Cheder · Jewish elementary school.

City College of New York · College attended by many immigrant Jews who were then able to work their way out of the poverty of the Lower East Side.

City Hall · The chief administrative building of a city.

Cohen, Morris Raphael (1880–1947) · Professor of philosophy at the City College of New York and later at the University of Chicago. Very influential among young Jewish immigrants. After 1933, deeply involved in research on Jewish problems.

Columbia University · One of the oldest universities in America. Admitted few Jewish students until the 1930s.

Communist Revolution · The overthrow of the Tsarist government by the Bolsheviks in 1917. Bolsheviks are also called "Communists" or "Reds."

Conservative Jew · One of three major Jewish groups in the United States, Conservative Judaism seeks a middle path between tradition and change, but emphasizes traditions wherever possible. A Conservative Jew is one who follows Conservative Judaism. The three major groups are Reform, Conservative, and Orthodox Judaism.

Cooper Union · Pioneer in tuition-free evening adult education. Founded in 1859 in New York City.

(The) crown of a good name · A statement in the Babylonian Talmud (Avot 4:17) reads: "Rabbi Shimon said: 'There are three crowns: the crown of Torah, the crown of priesthood, and the crown of kingdom; but the crown of a good name is better than all of them'." (See *Talmud* in glossary below for definition.)

Daven/Davening · The way Orthodox Jews pray, chanting prayers with a swaying motion.

David · Second king of Israel who lived approximately 950 B.C.E. It is claimed that he wrote the Book of Psalms in the Bible.

Dayan (im) · Judge(s) of the rabbinical court.

Democratic Party · The political party that dominated New York City politics and that was especially popular among immigrant groups.

Dubinsky, David (1892–1982) · Leader of the International Ladies Garment Workers' Union, the American Federation of Labor, and the Jewish Labor Committee.

Eastern European Jew · A Jew from Poland, Hungary, Czechoslovakia, Roumania, Russia, or smaller countries in the same region. Immigrants from this region numbered between 2.5 to 3 million between 1880 and 1925. They were generally poor Orthodox Jews who had a hard time adjusting to American life.

Educational Alliance · Opened in 1883, this school helped immigrants adjust to American ways and ideas.

Ellis Island · In New York Bay, it served from 1890 to 1954 as a federal immigration station and the place where most Eastern European Jews first set foot on American soil.

Faithful and Merciful Healer · A phrase from the eighth benediction of the central prayer of the daily morning religious service.

FBI · The Federal Bureau of Investigation investigates violations of federal law. Attempting to overthrow the government is such a violation.

Fleish! Frishe fleish! Glat kosher fleish! · Yiddish phrase meaning "Meat! Fresh meat! Strictly kosher meat!" (See *Kosher* below.)

Forvarts · The *Jewish Daily Forward,* a Yiddish newspaper, published in New York and edited by Abraham Cahan. Probably the most well-known and influential of such papers, it helped immigrants understand American life and adjust to it.

Freud, Dr. Sigmund (1856–1939) · Austrian Jew who founded psychoanalysis. He published many books about his theory which at first was not acceptable by many in the medical profession.

Ganze Macher · Yiddish phrase meaning "a big shot."

German Jew · Jew who came from Germany or Austria. About 150,000 such immigrants came to America between 1700 and 1850 and were well adjusted to American life by the time events in this book take place.

Gershwin, George (1898–1937) · Composer who combined jazz, cantorial, and other music into well-known works, such as *Rhapsody in Blue* and *Porgy and Bess.*

Gershwin, Ira (1896–1983) · Wrote lyrics for the music of his brother, George Gershwin, and other composers.

Gluck, Alma (1884–1938) · Opera singer who came to America as a child from Roumania and became a leading figure on the New York musical scene.

Grand Theatre · A major Yiddish theater on Grand Street, New York City.

Goldfaden, Abraham (1840–1908) · Immigrant from Russia, he led the Yiddish theater movement in New York as a producer, playwright, and composer.

Goldman, Emma (1869–1940) · Born in Lithuania, she came to the U.S. and led the anarchist movement which believed in overthrowing any government that sought to limit personal freedom. She was expelled from this country in 1919 as an undesirable alien.

Gompers, Samuel (1850–1924) · Founder and president of the American Federation of Labor after 1886. Worked diligently to improve the conditions of all workers.

Gordin, Jacob (1853–1909) · Left Russia in 1891 for America in search of greater religious freedom. Prolific playwright and translator for the Yiddish theater in New York.

Haftarah · A section of the biblical books of the prophets read every Sabbath in the synagogue.

Hammerstein, Oscar, II (1895–1960) · Wrote the words to many famous musicals, including *Oklahoma, South Pacific, The King and I,* and *The Sound of Music.*

Harlem · Before the influx of blacks, about 1910, it was a fashionable residential section of New York City.

Harmonie Club · Founded in 1852 by German-American Jews, the club provided educational and social activities. Later, it added a gymnasium and a country club on Long Island. It was and remains a center of Jewish leadership and affluence in New York City.

Hebrew Immigrant Aid Society (HIAS) · Begun in 1909, HIAS became the largest organization helping immigrants. Its representatives worked both in Europe and on Ellis Island in New York Harbor to assist Jewish travelers and to protect them from unscrupulous merchants and government officials. (See *Ellis Island* above.)

Henry Street Settlement House · A neighborhood house or center that provided education, counseling, recreation, and physical necessities (money, food, clothing, fuel, job placement, and health care) for the immigrant residents of the Lower East Side in New York.

Hillquit, Morris (1869–1933) · Leader of the Socialist party (see below) of America and advocate for better conditions for workers.

Holy Land · Another term for Palestine (today's Israel). So-called because Jews consider the land of this area especially blessed by God.

Ibrahim · Arabic form of Abraham.

International Institute of Agriculture (IIA) · Founded in 1905 by David Lubin in Rome, Italy, the IIA was intended to use scientific advances to improve agriculture in the seventy countries that belonged to it.

International Ladies Garment Workers' Union · Founded in 1900, it is the union representing workers who make women's clothing.

Jewish Institute of Religion · Reform Jewish rabbinical school, founded in 1922 in New York City by Rabbi Stephen S. Wise. Merged with Hebrew Union College in 1948.

Jewish Theological Seminary of America · Rabbinical school of the Conservative Jewish movement, located in New York City. (See *Conservative* above.)

(American Jewish) Joint Distribution Committee · Founded in 1914 to relieve the sufferings of European Jews after World War I. It has continued this helping role on a worldwide scale ever since.

Joseph, Jacob · To resolve the problems of an undisciplined American Jewry, fifteen Orthodox congregations invited Jacob Joseph, a distinguished European rabbi, to become chief rabbi of New York. This 1888 attempt failed when others would neither accept his authority nor pay the tax on kosher meat which was to support him. (See below definition of *kosher.*)

Kahn, Gus (1886–1941) · Song writer.

Kapulia · A typical shtetl (see below definition for *shtetl*) where regional fairs were held on market days. Many Jews left towns like this one and came to America between 1880 and 1924.

Kapulyer Farband · A landsmannschaft (see below) or society composed mostly of people from the area of Kapulia.

Kehillah · Hebrew word meaning "community." Between 1909 and 1922, New York City Jewry tried to manage its affairs with a democratically-elected government called the Kehillah. It worked to improve education, public welfare, community-police relations, employment, and to settle questions concerning religious practices and other disputes. It dissolved when New York's Jews could not agree on what powers the Kehillah should have.

Kibbutzim (Singular: Kibbutz) · Collective settlements in Palestine organized by European Jews. All decisions were made by collective vote, and property was owned in common. Today, kibbutzim are owned and operated by native-born Israelis.

Kiddush · The blessing over a cup of wine at the beginning of the Sabbath.

Knishes · Meat- or potato-filled pastry.

Kosher · Religiously or ritually proper for use. Usually refers to food which must be prepared in special ways.

Kuhn, Loeb and Company · A major investment banking company founded in 1867 by Abraham Kuhn and Solomon Loeb who had begun their careers as clothing merchants in Cincinnati, Ohio.

Landsmannschaft · A society of people from the same region who help each other, especially in times of personal financial emergency. An early form of mutual insurance company.

London, Meyer (1871–1926) · Lawyer and socialist leader who was elected to the United States House of Representatives in 1914; from the Lower East Side of New York.

Lubin, David (1849–1919) · Founder of the International Institute of Agriculture. Considered the world's best-known agricultural organizer and reformer.

Luftmenschen · Yiddish word meaning "Air persons." It refers both to intellectuals who talk a lot, but act very little, and to the homeless who have no means of support and who seem to live not on bread but on air.

Ma'ariv · Daily evening religious service.

(La) Marseillaise · The French national anthem. After the French Revolution of 1789, it became the theme song of many revolutionary movements. It was composed by Rouget de l'Isle in 1792.

Marshall, Louis (1856–1929) · Lawyer and communal leader. Chief spokesman for New York's German-Jewish elite who used his influence to protect Jewish rights around the world. Dedicated Jew and supporter of early efforts to make Palestine a center of Jewish settlement.

May 1 · Day on which the Communist Revolution is celebrated.

Messiah · Judaism teaches that God either through an agent (the Messiah) or directly will bring an end to human history and establish an era of perfection (the Messianic Age).

Mezuzah · A small case attached to the doorpost of a Jewish home, containing a tiny scroll of parchment on which the Shema and two paragraphs from Deuteronomy (6:4–9, 11:13–21) are written.

Milchik · Yiddish word meaning "food made only of dairy products."

Minchah · Daily afternoon religious service.

Mi Sheberach · Prayer recited to thank God.

Mishpachah · Hebrew for "family."

Mitzvot (Singular: Mitzvah) · Hebrew word meaning "God's commandments." Usually used to mean good deeds.

Mutual Alliance Trust Company · Located at 323-5 Grand Street, in New York City, this bank, through the American Federation of Zionists, represented the Jewish National Fund in America. Its board of directors included Jews together with Rockefellers and Vanderbilts.

National Farm School · Established in 1896 by Rabbi Joseph Krauskopf in Doylestown, Pennsylvania, the school trained immigrant Jewish youths in practical farming.

Neilah · Concluding service of Yom Kippur. (See *Yom Kippur* below.)

(The) New York Times · Newspaper which publisher Adolph S. Ochs (1858–1935) turned into one of the most influential papers in the country.

New York University · University located in the southern part of Manhattan and popular among Jews.

Nudnick · Yiddish word meaning "dope."

Orthodox Jew · A Jew who observes the religion in the most traditional manner.

Pale of Settlement · An area that today would include parts of western Russia, Poland, Hungary, Czechoslovakia, Roumania, and Bulgaria. By 1885, four million Jews had been forced to move into this area, and more were driven in later by anti-Semitic governments. Eastern European living conditions were terrible. The Pale of Settlement was legally abolished in 1917.

Pesach Seder · The religious service and meal celebrating Passover. Pesach is the Hebrew for Passover, the holiday commemorating the Exodus from Egypt.

Picon, Molly (1898–) · Actress on both the Yiddish and English stages.

Pogrom · An organized attack on helpless people. From 1871 to 1906, approximately 53 major pogroms were directed against Eastern European Jews, often with government help.

Ponselle, Rosa (1897–1981) · Opera singer.

Promised Land · According to the Bible (Genesis 13:14–17), God promised the area of Palestine to Abraham and his descendants forever.

Reform Jew · A liberal Jew who is willing to adapt Jewish customs to modern conditions.

Rishon Letzion · Founded in 1882, it was the first kibbutz (see definition above) established by pioneers from outside Palestine. Known for its grapes, wine, and citrus fruit. For the name, see Isaiah 41:27.

Rodgers, Richard (1902–1979) · Composer who wrote music for many famous shows, including *Carousel, Oklahoma, South Pacific, Annie Get Your Gun,* and *Sound of Music.* Often worked with Oscar Hammerstein II.

Scab · A worker hired by a company while regular workers are on strike. Scab labor undercut strikes and jeopardized union jobs.

Shabbat · Hebrew word for "Sabbath."

Shacharit · Daily morning religious service.

Shadchan · Hebrew and Yiddish word meaning "marriage arranger" or matchmaker.

Shalom · As a welcome greeting, it means "Hello."

Shehecheyanu · A blessing of thanksgiving recited on many important joyous occasions.

Shivah · The seven-day period of mourning after the death of a close relative.

Shtetl · A small town in the Pale of Settlement with a very large Jewish population. (See *Pale of Settlement* above.)

Shul · Yiddish word for "synagogue."

Siddur · Hebrew word for "prayer book."

Smithsonian Institution · The national museum of the United States, located in Washington, DC.

Socialism · Political and economic theory advocating government or communal ownership of business as opposed to capitalism which advocates private ownership.

Socialist Party · A political party popular among Eastern European workers which pushed for better conditions for workers and for greater government control of the economy.

Society for Ethical Culture · Founded by Felix Adler in 1876, it was an offshoot of Reform Judaism without the religious ceremonials and religious-ethnic commitments of traditional Judaism.

Solomon · Son of David, he was the third king of Israel and ruled from about 940 to 922 B.C.E. He is said to have been very wise and to have written many biblical works. The First Temple was built by Solomon.

**(The) study of wisdom is equal to all the rest of God's command-
ments** · The Mishnah (Peah 1:1), a book of Jewish law and
thought compiled in the Galilee about 200 C.E. by Judah Ha-Nasi
(Judah the Prince), describes some acts that are so important that
one should never stop doing them and others which gain rewards
in the world-to-come. But the Mishnah concludes that study is
more important even than all of these.

Sukot · The harvest festival described in Leviticus 23:33–36
and often called the Festival of Booths or Tabernacles.

Tageblatt · Yiddish Socialist daily newspaper founded in New
York City in 1885.

Talmud · The Babylonian Talmud (about 500 C.E.) contains the
Jewish laws of that period, legends, stories, and disputes and is
considered more authoritative than the Palestinian or Jerusalem
Talmud (about 450 C.E.). The Talmud still forms the basis for Orthodox Jewish practice.

Tammany Hall · A private political club which controlled New
York City politics by organizing a large number of immigrant vot-
ers on any issue. Though Tammany Hall did much good for the
poor immigrants (especially Irish and Jewish), scandal and fraud
were often connected with it. It was controlled by a single person
known as the "Boss."

Tayerhar Mishpocheh · Yiddish phrase meaning "Dear family."

Temple Emanu-El · Founded in 1845, this congregation became
the largest Reform Jewish temple in the world and was the center
of German-Jewish or uptown-Jewish life in New York City. Today,
it is called Congregation Emanu-El.

Tenement · An apartment building, usually in poor condition and with bad ventilation, common on the Lower East Side of New York.

Thomashefsky, Boris (1868–1939) · Actor and director in the Yiddish theater.

Tin Pan Alley · The area along 28th Street where Jewish and non-Jewish composers, singers, and musicians gathered and worked.

Torah · The scroll—containing Genesis, Exodus, Leviticus, Numbers, and Deuteronomy—which is read weekly in the synagogue and studied constantly. Also refers generally to Jewish teaching and wisdom.

Treif · Yiddish word meaning "not kosher" or religiously not acceptable.

Triangle Shirtwaist Company · A sweatshop in New York's Washington Square. In March 1911, a fire killed 146 workers. This tragedy made many people more aware of the terrible conditions in the sweatshops and, eventually, led to some improvements.

Tsar · Title held by the ruler of Russia before 1917.

Tsedakah · Hebrew word meaning "charity."

Two Kitchens · Orthodox Jews do not mix milk and meat products. Therefore, they prepare these foods in separate kitchens.

Union Temple · A Reform Jewish temple in Brooklyn.

Uptown/Downtown · Jews who lived uptown were usually middle and upper class and of German background. Downtown Jews were poorer, newer residents from Eastern Europe and more Orthodox. Uptowners did not respect downtowners.

Uvacharta Ba-Chayim · "And you shall choose life." (Deuteronomy 30:19)

Victor Emanuel II (1820–1878) · King of Italy, sponsored the creation of the International Institute of Agriculture and invited David Lubin to head it. The goal was scientific study of agriculture to produce more food for the world's hungry.

Wald, Lillian (1867–1940) · Social worker and nurse who established the Henry Street Settlement House in New York to care for the needs of Jewish immigrants. She campaigned for an end to child labor, the outlawing of war, the promotion of unions, and other social reforms.

Warburg · A family of German-American Jewish bankers and leaders in Jewish and civic causes. The best-known in the family was Felix (1871–1937).

Warren, Leonard (1911–1960) · Opera singer.

Weisenfreund, Muni (1895–1967) · Also known as Paul Muni, star of Yiddish theater, Broadway, and Hollywood.

Western Wall · Also known as the Wailing Wall. The only remnant of the Jerusalem Temple, it is the object of traditional Jewish pilgrimages. Jews gather at the Wall for prayer.

Wise, Stephen S. (1874–1949) · Reform Jewish rabbi and Zionist leader; founder of the Jewish Institute of Religion; active in many Jewish, civic, and political causes.

"Workers of the world, unite" · Slogan used by the Communists.

World War I · Between 1914 and 1918, war ravaged most of Europe. It was particularly devastating for Jews in the Pale of Settlement. (See *Pale of Settlement* above.)

Yekum Purkan · Ancient prayer for the welfare of scholars, leaders, and the congregation.

Yiddish (Adjective: Yiddishe) · A language which mixes medieval German, Hebrew, and Slavic words and which became the daily language of most European Jews. The Yiddish adjective is used to refer to anything Jewish.

Yom Kippur · The Day of Atonement, one of the two High Holy Days, is the most solemn occasion of the Jewish calendar. It is a day of fast and repentance.

Zionism · Movement to secure the return of the Jews to Israel.

Zionists · Persons who support a Jewish homeland in Palestine, either by donations or by moving there.